P9-CBC-660

SHIPWRECK!

A *SURVIVE!* Story

BY JAKE MADDOX

illustrated by Sean Tiffany

text by Marc Tyler Nobleman

STONE ARCH BOOKS
www.stonearchbooks.com

Impact Books are published by Stone Arch Books,
A Capstone Imprint
151 Good Counsel Drive, P.O. Box 669
Mankato, Minnesota 56002
www.capstonepub.com

Library of Congress Cataloging-in-Publication Data
Maddox, Jake.
Shipwreck! A Survive! Story / by Jake Maddox; illustrated by Sean Tiffany.
p. cm. — (Impact Books. A Jake Maddox Sports Story)
ISBN 978-1-4342-1207-8 (library binding)
ISBN 978-1-4342-1405-8 (pbk.)
[1. Shipwrecks—Fiction. 2. Survival—Fiction.] I. Tiffany, Sean, ill. II. Title.
PZ7.M25643Sh 2009
[Fic]—dc22 2008031961

Summary:
When their whale-watching trip goes horribly wrong, Skylar, Gabby, and Miles find themselves on an inflatable raft in the middle of the ocean. With no food, a small amount of water, and only a small first-aid kit to help them, they must spend three treacherous days on the waves, hoping desperately for help to arrive. Sharks circle, their water supply dwindles, and Gabby begins to hallucinate. Will they survive, or are they lost at sea forever?

Creative Director: Heather Kindseth
Graphic Designer: Carla Zetina-Yglesias

Printed in the United States of America in Stevens Point, Wisconsin.
032010
005721R

TABLE OF CONTENTS

CHAPTER 1

Killers at Sea

Fourteen-year-old Gabby Moore glared down at the ocean. She said, "Since I haven't seen any whales, do you think the whales are hiding out there, watching us?"

She whirled around. Her friend Skylar laughed. Miles, Gabby's 16-year-old brother, smirked. Gabby could tell that he was trying not to laugh. When Skylar glanced at Miles, he walked to the other side of the boat.

"You knew there might not be anything," Gabby's mother said.

"Captain Steve can't promise that we'll see whales," their father said.

"I've been taking folks out on the *Gusto* for twenty-two years," Captain Steve said, patting the railing of the boat. "In all that time, the people sure have changed, but the animals haven't. They're still as hard to find as they were when I started."

He pointed to a vinyl banner that hung on the boat. "Whale They or Won't They Show Up?" was printed on it in silver letters. There was a cartoon picture of a whale winking.

"Just like the poster says, Gabby," Captain Steve said. "The whales will show up if they feel like it."

Captain Steve was friends with Gabby's mom. Recently, Gabby's science teacher had assigned the class to do projects about different animals. Gabby and Skylar got whales. Gabby's mom called Captain Steve, who agreed to take the Moores and Skylar out on his boat.

"It's okay, Gabby," Skylar said. "We don't need to see live whales to do a great job. After all, Gina and Rachel won't be looking in the woods for black bears."

"That's right," Gabby's mother said. Then she sighed. "Girls, it's 80 degrees outside. Please put on more sunscreen."

Gabby rolled her eyes, but she put some sunscreen on her face and bare legs. Then she checked her watch. They'd been on the boat for an hour and hadn't seen a single whale. That was a bad sign.

She sighed and walked over to where Miles was standing. “I can’t decide what’s more boring about this,” Gabby said. “Being stuck on a whale-watching trip without whales, or being stuck on a boat all day with you.”

“Don’t take this out on me,” Miles said. “It’s not my fault the whales don’t like us.”

“Mom said you could’ve stayed home,” Gabby said.

“I came for research,” Miles told her. “Not like your little school project. Real research.”

“Oh, I forgot,” Gabby said. “This is your first official mission as a lifeguard.”

“I didn’t know you passed your lifeguard test,” Skylar said as she walked up behind them.

"He needed a change from his first two tries," Gabby said.

"That's really cool, Miles," Skylar said, ignoring Gabby and smiling at Miles. "Congratulations."

"Hey, kids, come check this out!" Gabby's dad yelled. He was pointing off the side of the boat. "That's a whale, isn't it?" he asked.

Everyone headed over, including Captain Steve and the first mate, Holly.

"Wow," Holly said. "I've never seen one of those in the wild before."

"It's beautiful," Captain Steve said as the glossy black and white animal came close to breaking the surface. "It's an orca. A killer whale."

"Killer whale?" Miles asked. "Around here?"

Skylar took out her digital camera. She snapped photos.

"What's that?" Gabby asked. "Another one?" She pointed toward something large swimming several yards away from the first one. Both animals were headed toward the *Gusto*. Fast.

"It looks like they're following the boat," Mom said.

Captain Steve frowned. "Everyone away from the edge," he said. Gabby had never heard him sound so nervous before.

The group did as they were told. Dad stood on his tiptoes so that he could see over the side of the boat. "That looks like a third one," he said.

Gabby heard a loud splintering sound. The 36-foot-long boat lurched forward. Everybody screamed.

"What's happening?" Gabby shrieked.

"The whales are attacking the boat!" Captain Steve said. He stuffed a waterproof pack of flares into a vest pocket.

Gabby's mom grabbed some life preservers from a stack. She threw them at Gabby, Miles, and Skylar, who put them on.

"It's okay," Captain Steve said. "Orcas do that sometimes. As long as they don't hit us again, we'll be fine."

Another hit made the boat rock. Jets of water, mixed with pieces of wood, shot up. Everyone was thrown around the deck. Gabby's dad slid hard into a railing. Skylar bumped her knee on a bench.

Captain Steve and Holly stood up quickly. They ran to a large canister that was attached to a wall of the boat. Together, they heaved it overboard.

When it hit the water, the canister split open and a red piece of fabric burst out. Then the fabric filled with air. In seconds, it inflated into a four-person life raft. It looked like a small castle. It even had a small boarding ramp.

"We have to abandon ship!" Captain Steve shouted. The boat shook as the orcas rammed into it a third time. "Now!"

CHAPTER 2

Goodbye to the *Gusto*

Captain Steve grabbed Gabby and Skylar's wrists and pulled them to the railing. "It'll be okay," he said. "I'll go with you."

Holly helped Miles, Mom, and Dad toward the railing. Captain Steve and the girls jumped. They hit the ocean. Gabby went underwater at first, but her life preserver quickly brought her back up to the surface.

Captain Steve helped boost them into the raft. He turned back to the boat to see Gabby's parents, Miles, and Holly leap over the railing.

Miles nearly landed on top of the life raft. Once Miles had climbed into the raft with Skylar and Gabby, Captain Steve pulled out a small knife from his pocket. He sliced the cord that connected the raft to the *Gusto*. The raft floated away from the ship. Captain Steve swam toward the other three passengers.

Pieces of the ship spilled into the sea. Chunks of metal and plastic floated on the surface for a moment before disappearing into the water. Gabby saw her parents cling to a large piece of wood. Holly held onto another piece of wood as Captain Steve swam up to them.

The ocean began to suck the *Gusto* down. The force of the water churning around the ship pushed the kids and the adults farther from each other. Captain Steve grabbed onto the wood Holly was holding. Dad started to swim toward the kids, but Captain Steve yelled, "No! You'll never make it!"

With a loud whoosh, the *Gusto* tipped upright. Then the boat sank.

Gabby felt like a big snake was squeezing her stomach as she watched her parents float farther away from her. A red flare rocketed up from near them.

"Mom! Dad!" Gabby called. They yelled something back, but it sounded like nonsense, like voices on a cell phone about to lose its signal.

Gabby and Skylar called out again. In a few minutes, they had screamed their throats raw. But the adults were still floating away. Soon, they had disappeared.

Miles put his hand on his sister's arm. "They'll be fine," he said. "They've got Captain Steve."

"What about us?" Gabby asked quietly.

"We've got a raft," Miles said.

"And a lifeguard," Skylar said, looking at Miles.

Tears trickled down Gabby's face and fell into the ocean.

CHAPTER 3

Three Alone

Miles squinted out at the sea. Gabby and Skylar huddled under the raft's canopy. The only thing keeping them from freaking out was the hope that someone had seen Captain Steve's flare and would be cruising by any minute to pick them up.

Though the sun had dried them off quickly, they still felt a chill. A cool breeze blew on them, and the raft floor they sat on was covered in puddles of water.

"How could they drift a different way than us?" Gabby asked. She shook her head. Then she asked quietly, "Do you think the killer whales will come back?"

Miles looked out at the horizon. He didn't say anything. Skylar was quiet too. She just looked down at her arms and legs. She was covered in scratches and bruises from the attack and escape.

"You guys," Gabby said. "Are you listening?"

"Let's focus on how we can get through this," Miles said. "We can't get distracted by questions we won't be able to figure out."

"Oh, is that what you've been doing for the past hour?" Gabby asked. "Focusing on getting through this? Because it looks like the only thing you've been focusing on is the horizon."

"I'm trying to think," Miles said.

"So what have you come up with?" Gabby asked.

Miles slid down the low, squishy wall of the raft. "Nothing," he admitted. "Yet."

Gabby frowned at her brother. "Our phones are wrecked, right?" she asked.

All three of them pulled their phones out of their pockets. All three phones were soaked, and none of them would turn on.

"Well, I guess we can't call for help," Gabby said. Then she stood up and screamed, "HELP!"

"Save your voice for when there's someone who can hear it," Miles said.

"HELP! HELP!" Gabby yelled.

"Will you stop?" Miles said.

"HELP!" Gabby yelled again. Her throat was starting to hurt.

"Seriously, Gabby, cut it out," Miles said.

"GABRIELA AND MILES MOORE!" Skylar screamed.

Gabby and Miles turned to look at her. "Whoa. What?" Gabby asked.

"I've come up with something," Skylar said. "A name."

Miles frowned. "A name for what?" he asked.

"A name for our ship," Skylar said.

"Our ship?" Miles repeated. "What are you talking about?"

"What's the name?" Gabby asked.

"*Tub,*" Skylar said, smiling.

"Okay, I may not know what we should be doing, but I am pretty sure that naming the raft is not important," Miles said, rolling his eyes.

Gabby ignored him. "Why *Tub*?" she asked.

"You know, the old nursery rhyme. It goes like, 'Rub-a-dub-dub, three men in a tub,' blah blah blah, something about sailing out to sea," Skylar explained, smiling.

No one spoke for a moment. Finally, Gabby asked, "Then can I be the candlestick maker?"

Gabby and Skylar laughed. After a few seconds, Miles laughed too.

"And that's why we need a name," Skylar said.

Miles stood up and clapped his hands. "All right," he said. "First things first. Let's get this ship in shape. Let's get this water out of here."

With their hands, the three kids scooped water over the edge of the raft. Soon, the floor puddles were gone.

Then Miles spotted something long and white floating their way. "Look, the banner from the ship," he said. They paddled toward it and pulled the banner aboard. They read the words again: "Whale They or Won't They Show Up?"

"That is the question of the day," Miles said. "So what do you think? Whale they show up? And I'm not really talking about the whales, you know."

"We know," Skylar said.

"They will show up," Gabby said.

Skylar nodded. "Someone will save us," she said.

"Right answer," Miles said.

CHAPTER 4

Flashes of Light

Gabby noticed a fabric pack stuck onto the side of the raft's wall. It was attached with Velcro. She tore it off and turned it over. When she read the label, she yelled, "Hey!"

"What?" Miles asked.

"This is a pack of emergency supplies!" Gabby told him. She shook the bag open and let the contents spill out.

The bag contained flares, a knife, six small packages of drinking water, two little paddles, a whistle, a flashlight, a mirror, a fishing kit, a first aid kit, and a few other things the kids didn't recognize.

Miles picked up the whistle and blew on it. Then he put it down again.

"There's no food," Gabby said after looking at everything in the bag.

"It doesn't matter," Miles said. "We won't be here long enough to get too hungry."

He looked at the horizon. As the sun sank, the sky was turning bright red.

"It'll be dark soon," Skylar said. "Do you think they'll find us before that?"

"I think they will," Gabby said. She turned to look at the ocean.

"It doesn't feel like we've drifted that far since we lost sight of Mom and Dad," she added. She tried to sound brave, but she felt like crying.

"I think we should shoot off one of these flares. Then we should try to relax. We need to save our energy," Miles said.

"Shouldn't we wait until it's dark to shoot off a flare? Or until we see a ship or a plane?" Skylar asked. "We only have three flares."

"Yeah, that's a better idea," Gabby said.

"Captain Steve fired one right away," Miles said.

"Captain Steve didn't have a raft," Gabby said.

"I'm the oldest," Miles said. "I'll make the decisions."

"Being the oldest doesn't make you the ship's captain," Gabby told him, rolling her eyes.

"We're wasting time," Miles said. He took out a flare. "I'm going to set one off."

Quickly, Gabby reached out. She tried to grab the flare from Miles.

"Hey!" Miles yelled. "Quit it!"

The two fought for the flare for a second. It slipped out of their hands, bounced on the edge of the raft, and fell into the sea.

"No!" Miles and Gabby shouted. Miles leaned over the edge of the raft and reached for it, but the flare was already underwater.

"Great," Miles said to Gabby. "You wanted to be the candlestick maker. Can you make us another one of those?"

"Maybe I should be in charge of the supplies," Skylar said quietly.

Gabby and Skylar sat under the canopy in one corner of the raft. Miles sat in the opposite corner.

Gabby took her MP3 player out of the zippered pocket in her windbreaker and stuck one of the earbuds in her ear. "Still works!" she said, smiling. She handed the other earbud to Skylar. Miles tipped his head back against the canopy wall. As the upper sky began to darken, all three of them fell asleep.

* * *

Hours later, a crack of thunder jolted them awake. Gabby looked at her watch, but it was too dark out. She couldn't see anything.

Skylar fumbled her way to the supplies. She found the flashlight, and switched it on. "It's 10 o'clock," she said. "Should we set off a flare?"

A bolt of lightning ripped through the sky. All three kids screamed.

"We can set off a flare when the storm passes," Miles said. "If that's okay with you," he added, glaring at his sister.

Thunder shook the sky again, louder than before. The wind had picked up. The raft bounced up and down on the waves. Water was spilling over the sides.

"Good thing we don't have anything in our stomachs," Skylar said. "This would definitely make us sick!"

Miles took off his shoe. He used it to dump out water.

He worked faster and faster, but he couldn't keep up with all the water pouring into the boat. A bolt of lightning zigzagged down the sky.

"You said we should save our energy!" Skylar called.

"Yeah, for times like this!" Miles said.

"You're going to wear yourself out!" Gabby said. "Let's just try to wait!"

Miles emptied a few more shoefuls of water. Then he gave up. It started to rain. The canopy began to vibrate when the raindrops hit it. Thunder rolled over the sky. All three kids were shivering. Each one was silently hoping that help would hurry up and come.

CHAPTER 5

Teeth

Gabby heard the gentle sloshing of water against the raft. As long as she kept her eyes closed, there was still a chance it was all just a bad dream.

"The *Tub* made it through the night," Skylar said. "So did we."

Morning light came through the canopy flaps. Gabby opened her eyes and blinked at the strong sun. Skylar was clicking the flashlight on and off.

"But the flashlight was not as lucky," Skylar added, smiling.

"There are spare batteries in the supplies," Miles said. "But from now on, we shouldn't leave it on unless we have to."

Something buzzed outside. Miles flung open the canopy flaps. He stuck his head out and looked up.

"A plane!" he yelled. "Quick! Give me a flare!"

Gabby grabbed one of the flares and handed it to Miles. He quickly read the directions printed on the side of the flare. Then he tossed it into the air. All three kids screamed and waved their arms, hoping someone would see them.

Gabby muttered, "Please, please, please, please!"

The plane kept going by. For a moment, it looked as though it was turning to circle them. It didn't. It just kept flying the same direction it had been heading.

Miles sank sadly to the floor of the ramp. The plane shrank to the size of a dot.

Gabby glanced at the last flare they had. "Maybe the pilot saw the flare," Gabby said. "Maybe he called for help."

"Maybe," Miles said. His stomach gurgled. "Maybe we could try to catch a fish in the meantime."

"I hate fish," Gabby said.

"Well, we can't exactly order pizzas," Miles said. "And we have to eat."

"We don't even know how to fish," Gabby said.

Skylar shuddered. "I like fish, but I don't think I could kill one," she said.

"Just let me try," Miles said. "Maybe it's not that hard." He took out the fishing kit. He attached one of the little metal hooks to the fishing line.

Miles peered over the edge of the raft. "I see some fish!" he said, smiling. He carefully tossed the hook into the water.

"Here, fishy, fishy, fishy," Skylar said quietly.

A few fish inspected the bait. None swam close enough to take it.

"Don't wait," Miles said. "Bite that bait." Gabby rolled her eyes at the silly rhyme.

Finally, a foot-long fish swam up. It chomped on the bait. Miles yanked on the line. The fish let go.

"Shoot!" Miles said. He dropped the line back into the water.

A few minutes later, another fish swam up to the hook and latched on. Miles pulled fast on the line. Suddenly, the fish was flopping on the floor of the raft.

"You did it!" Skylar said. They all cheered.

"What now?" Gabby said. "Do we just watch it die?"

Miles shrugged. "I guess so," he said.

The fish flopped around. Miles reached down, trying to make sure it didn't bounce out of the raft.

"Ow!" he yelled. He pulled his hand away. Gabby saw blood on his finger. "That thing has teeth!" Miles said.

Skylar unwrapped a bandage from the first aid kit. Miles put it on his hand.

Gabby cleaned the red drops of blood off the raft. "Ew, it looks like some got in the water," she said.

"Gross," Skylar said.

Just then, a surge of water shook the raft. Gabby screamed. She fell over the edge of the raft and into the water.

"Gabby!" Miles shouted. He moved toward the edge of the raft. He tried to grab his sister, but she was already too far away.

"Can you swim to us?" Skylar called.

Gabby didn't say anything. She knew how to swim, but she was panicking.

Then Miles and Skylar saw a dark shadow swim beneath her.

"Miles, is that what I think it is?" Skylar asked quietly.

Miles clamped his hand over her mouth. "Don't freak out," he said in a firm whisper. Then he removed his hand. Skylar nodded and covered her mouth with her own trembling hands.

Gabby didn't know there was a shark swimming below her. She stopped panicking and started to swim toward the raft. When she was ten feet away, her foot touched the shark.

She didn't see it, but she knew what it was. She stopped swimming and began to spin around. She slapped the water with her hands. "Get away!" she yelled.

Miles took a deep breath. Then he jumped into the water.

"Don't splash!" Skylar called out. "Stay calm!"

Gabby didn't listen. She didn't notice that Miles was swimming toward her. She was too scared.

Miles slowly swam up to his sister from behind. She was still slapping the water. When she heard Miles behind her, she screamed.

Miles swam up and put his arm across her chest. "It's okay, Gabby," he said quietly. "I'm going to help you, but you have to stop moving so much."

The shark bumped Miles in the shin. Miles took a deep breath. Slowly, he began to pull Gabby to the raft.

Standing on the raft, Skylar whispered, "Hurry!"

Then Skylar had an idea. She took off one of her shoes and hurled it as hard as she could. It flew over the shark and away from Miles and Gabby. But the shark didn't chase it.

Miles reached the raft. He didn't have much strength left. He pushed Gabby up, while Skylar pulled her into the raft by her arms. Once she was safely in the raft, Gabby curled up under the canopy.

Skylar tried to help Miles climb in, but he was too heavy. "Gabby, I need your help!" Skylar called.

Gabby didn't say anything, but she came over and helped pull Miles in. Just as Miles fell onto the floor of the raft, the shark leapt out of the water, snapping at the air. They all shrieked and scooted back. The shark disappeared.

Skylar sat down and took a deep breath. "Are you guys okay?" she asked quietly. Miles and Gabby both looked scared and seasick.

"Yeah," Miles said, panting. "I'm okay. Are you okay, Gabby?"

Gabby nodded. She didn't say anything.

Skylar looked out at the ocean. After a few moments, she asked, "Do you think it's gone?"

Miles shrugged. "I hope so," he said. "Hey, nice try with the shoe," he added, smiling gently. "At least we know it's not a dog shark."

"Miles," Gabby said softly. "You jumped in. I can't believe it. You got me."

Miles looked down and smiled again.

Gabby went on, "Thank you. I won't joke about you being a lifeguard ever again." She hugged Miles tightly.

"No, you can," Miles said. "I'm not."

The girls looked puzzled. "What do you mean?" Skylar asked.

"I lied," Miles said. "I didn't pass the test to become a lifeguard. Not even the third time."

Gabby hugged him again. "You passed today," she told him. "You saved my life."

CHAPTER 6

Down Here

After they rested for a while, all three kids felt a little better. "I'm starving," Skylar said finally. "I guess we should deal with this fish, huh?"

Using the knife from the emergency kit, Skylar scraped the scales off the fish. She laid it to dry in the afternoon sun. "I guess this makes me the baker," she said

"Which means I'm the butcher, since I caught the fish," Miles said.

Gabby looked over at the fish and gagged. “Gross,” she said. “Hamburgers would be about the best thing in the world right now.”

“Well, rescue would be the best thing in the world,” Skylar said. “But hamburgers are a close second.”

“How are we going to cook the fish?” Gabby asked.

“We’re not,” Miles said. “We’ll let it dry in the sun.”

“That’s disgusting,” Gabby said. “There’s no way I’ll eat that.”

Miles frowned. “Gabby, you have to eat something,” he said. “Anyway, people have been eating fish dried in the sun for thousands of years. It’s perfectly safe. Really.”

Gabby looked at Skylar. "Are you going to try it?" Gabby asked.

Skylar shrugged. "I don't think I have a choice," she said. "I'd rather eat something gross than starve to death."

"We'll have to leave it for a while, though," Miles told the girls. "It has to dry out really well."

"Can we have something to drink while we wait?" Skylar asked.

Miles frowned. "We have some water, but we don't have very much," he said. "We'll have to be careful with it. You can have a little bit now, and then we can have more in a few hours. We should try to save as much as we can."

"You're really sunburned," Gabby said, noticing her brother's pink skin.

Skylar laughed. "You are too, Gabby," she said. "I think we all are. We should've listened to your mom and put on way more sunscreen."

"Now you must be kicking yourself big time that you didn't stay home," Gabby said to Miles. She paused, then added, "Why did you come, really?"

"I told you already," Miles said. "Research."

"Since when are you into the ocean?" Gabby asked. "We went to Marine Planet and you sat on a bench with your face in a comic book the whole time."

"First of all, it was a graphic novel," Miles said. "And secondly, I'm not doing research about the ocean. I'm doing research about you."

"What do you mean?" Gabby asked. "What kind of research about me?"

Miles explained, "We used to be best friends. Now that we're older, most of the time we just bug each other. We barely even know each other anymore. So Mom said I should go somewhere with you where we wouldn't be busy with soccer practice and phone calls and IMing."

Gabby smiled. "I guess Mom didn't plan on a shipwreck," she said.

Miles shook his head and smiled. "Nope," he said.

"I'm sorry, Miles," Gabby said. "Sorry I've snapped at you so much."

"Come on, guys," Skylar said. "You're making me wish my annoying brother was here."

Gabby and Miles laughed.

* * *

For the rest of the afternoon, Gabby, Miles, and Skylar tried hard to ignore their surroundings. They slept a little, talked, and watched the sky.

Soon, the sky turned dark. Miles fell asleep.

"Tonight seems colder than last night," Skylar said.

Gabby nodded. "I know," she said. "It does."

Somehow, they fell asleep.

In the middle of the night, Miles opened his eyes. Both girls were asleep.

As he stared at the starry sky, Miles realized what had woken him up.

One of the stars was making a sound.

It was moving. And it was red.

"Another plane!" Miles shouted. He flipped on the flashlight and waved it wildly. "Gabby, the flare!" he yelled.

Gabby woke up and jumped to her feet. She grabbed the last flare and set it off. "Hey! We're down here!" she yelled.

Skylar had woken up too. She looked around, trying to find another way to help.

Suddenly, an idea flashed into her head. She found the banner from Captain Steve's boat and opened it up. Then she grabbed the flashlight from Miles.

Skylar aimed the flashlight at the silver words printed on the banner. The shiny letters reflected the light, creating a glimmering, eight-foot-long SOS.

"I think it's coming back!" Gabby yelled.

But the sound of the plane's engine faded. A moment later, it was gone.

CHAPTER 7

Found at Sea

It was hard to fall back asleep that night, but Gabby, Miles, and Skylar were exhausted enough that they finally slept. In the morning, they woke up starving.

Miles tried to eat a strip of the dried fish, but the taste almost made him throw up.

"We can't eat this," he said. "I don't think it's safe." He looked like he was going to cry. Then he tossed the fish overboard.

As the hours went on, Gabby began to cough more and more. Skylar's sunburn hurt really badly, and it was starting to blister.

All three of them were moving very slowly. More than half of their water was gone.

"Look!" Gabby said, sitting up. She pointed at the sky with a shaky finger. "Who knew flamingos lived this far north?" she asked. "Or do you think we floated all the way down to Florida?"

Miles and Skylar looked where she was pointing. There were no birds of any kind.

"Either way, if they're here," Gabby said, "we must be near land."

"You should try to sleep," Miles told Gabby.

Gabby lay back down, but didn't close her eyes. She just stared up at the sky.

Skylar looked upset. "Gabby is seeing things," she whispered to Miles. "I'm really worried about her."

"Me too," Miles said quietly.

"There's another one," Gabby said, pointing again.

Miles didn't look up. Skylar peered into the bright sky. Then she gasped. "Look, Miles!" Skylar said.

Miles rolled his eyes. "You're seeing things too, huh?" he said.

"No, really, look!" Skylar shouted.

Miles looked up. His eyes were wide when he saw the plane. He whispered, "They found us."

This time, none of them shouted or waved. They just waited.

Within five minutes, the small plane landed on the ocean, not far from the raft. The door swung open and a man stuck his head out.

"You must be Miles, Skylar, and Gabby," he called. "Your parents sent me to get you."

He threw a rope to the raft. Miles grabbed it and tied it to the raft. Then the man pulled the raft to the plane.

"So our parents are alive," Miles said. He smiled and hugged his sister. Gabby smiled too.

"Yes, they're fine," the pilot said. "They were picked up an hour after the ship went down." He smiled.

"But of course they have been worried sick about you," the pilot added. "Now, climb into the plane. My name's Jack, by the way."

One by one, the kids took Jack's hand. They each climbed into the small airplane.

"How'd you find us?" Miles asked once everyone was inside.

"Another pilot saw your signal last night," Jack told them. "They sent out five planes looking for you. I'm really sorry it took so long. The ocean can push a raft miles away in less time than you'd think. Well, you're safe now."

"Where are our parents?" Gabby asked quietly.

"They're back at your house, waiting," Jack said.

"Will you take us to them?" Gabby asked.

"We'll take you to the hospital first," Jack said. "Make sure you're all right. But your parents will meet us there. Now try to stay quiet and relax. We'll be there soon."

As the plane rose above the water, the kids glanced down at *Tub*. It had been their home for the past 68 hours.

Skylar waved at it. "What about the raft?" she asked.

"I'll radio the boat to come get it," Jack said. Then he added, "You must be starving."

"Yes. For anything," Miles said. "Even pineapple pizza."

"This is all I have, but we'll be on land in no time," Jack said.

He handed them a box of crackers. They were shaped like little orange goldfish.

"Of all the food in the world, it had to be fish, didn't it?" Gabby said. She laughed.

In less than a minute, the box was empty.

Marc Tyler Nobleman has written books on everything from ghosts to Groundhog Day, belly flops to the Battle of the Little Bighorn, Superman to summertime activities. Besides writing books, he is also a cartoonist whose work has appeared in more than 100 magazines. He has never been through a real disaster but is living proof that it is possible to survive a bad hairdo.

ABOUT THE ILLUSTRATOR

When Sean Tiffany was growing up, he lived on a small island off the coast of Maine. Every day, from sixth grade until he graduated from high school, he had to take a boat to get to school. When Sean isn't working on his art, he works on a multimedia project called "OilCan Drive," which combines music and art. He has a pet cactus named Jim.

abandon (uh-BAN-duhn)—to leave forever

canister (KAN-ih-stur)—a container

captain (KAP-tin)—the person in charge of a ship

first mate (FURST MAYT)—a ship captain's assistant

flare (FLAIR)—a device that produces a bright light or flame as a signal

life preserver (LIFE pri-ZURV-er)—a belt, vest, or ring that can be filled with air and used to keep a person afloat in water

mission (MISH-uhn)—a special job or task

orca (OR-kuh)—a large, black and white whale. Orcas are also called killer whales.

research (REE-surch)—study or investigation about something

SOS (ESS OH ESS)—a signal meaning someone is in need of urgent help

In 1972, the Robertson family was enjoying a trip around the world. The family of six had been safely sailing for a year and a half. They had no idea what was in store for them.

One day, a group of killer whales rammed into the family's boat. Their boat sank beneath the surface in less than a minute. The family and a crew member scrambled to a life raft and a dinghy.

The food and water in the life raft was only enough for three days. The seven survived by eating flying fish and sea turtles. They drank rain water. As days turned into weeks, they used their imaginations to keep themselves busy.

For example, they imagined opening a restaurant. They even planned the entire menu.

Finally after 38 days lost at sea, the family was rescued. They were picked up by a Japanese fishing boat.

BE PREPARED FOR THE WORST

A well-stocked life raft emergency kit will have:

- flares and signaling mirrors
- drinking water
- a fishing kit
- sunscreen
- a first-aid kit

DISCUSSION QUESTIONS

1. Have you read other books or seen movies or TV shows about people who were lost at sea? Talk about the other stories you've heard.
2. What are some skills that would be good to have if you were shipwrecked? What are some skills that would not be helpful?
3. Gabby and Skylar wanted to go on Captain Steve's boat to learn more about whales. What are some other ways they could have learned about whales?

WRITING PROMPTS

1. If you were shipwrecked and had to live on a raft for three days, what five items would you want to have with you? Make a list and explain your reasons for each item.
2. Gabby was stuck on the raft with her brother and her best friend. If you were stuck on a raft, who would you want to be with? Write about that person.
3. At the end of this book, the three kids are safely headed home. What do you think happens next? Write about it!

OTHER BOOKS

Owen and Gray are stranded in the middle of a raging blizzard. Once the storm subsides, the boys decide to try to find their way back to civilization. Can they make it safely home, or will the frozen elements become too much for them to handle?

BY JAKE MADDOX

Ever since he arrived at his family's rented summer house, Brendan has been hearing horror stories about sharks in the water. Then, one day, when he's surfing off the coast, Brendan's shark nightmare comes true in a horrible way . . .

Do you want to know more about subjects related to this book? Or are you interested in learning about other topics? Then check out FactHound, a fun, easy way to find Internet sites.

Our investigative staff has already sniffed out great sites for you!

Here's how to use FactHound:

1. Visit *www.facthound.com*

2. Select your grade level.

3. To learn more about subjects related to this book, type in the book's ISBN number: **9781434212078**.

4. Click the **Fetch It** button.

FactHound will fetch the best Internet sites for you!